Princess Camomile
Gets Her Way

by Hiawyn Oram

illustrated by Susan Varley

Myriad Books

For Lara – H.O.

MYRIAD BOOKS LIMITED
35 Bishopsthorpe Road, London SE26 4PA

First published by
Andersen Press
20 Vauxhall Bridge Road
London SW1V 2SA
www.andersenpress.co.uk

ISBN 1 904 736 85 8

Printed in China

Camomile was a princess with a problem. Her nanny, Nanny Nettle, didn't allow this, she didn't allow that. She didn't allow her to go without her tiara or wear her old clothes. She didn't allow her to ride her new bike beyond the castle walls and she *never* allowed Camomile to eat sweets - even at her own birthday parties!

One morning Camomile woke up early.
"Enough is enough!" she said. "I'm just Not-Allowed!"
She pulled on some old shorts and a T-shirt.

She crept past Nanny Nettle's room.

She ran behind the gardener's back, and got out her bike.
Then she opened the secret door in the castle walls
no-one knew she knew how to open . . .

and pedalled out into the big wide world.
"Now," she said, "all I need is a sweet shop!"
And as soon as she turned a corner, there it was —
Bagseye the Bad Cat's Sweet Shop.
Inside, Bagseye was stroking his greasy whiskers,
over his greasy newspaper and wondering,
not for the first time, how bad a bad cat could be.

"Do you know?" he purred in his greasy purr
as Camomile stepped into the shop.
"Know what?" said Camomile.
"How bad a bad cat can be?" purred Bagseye.
"Eat a lot of these," said Camomile, waving round
at the sweets. "They're not allowed!"
"Oh, but they *are* allowed! As many as you like,
if you can pay for them," purred Bagseye.
"Here's a bag!"

"Thank you," said Camomile, taking the bag.
"But I can't pay for anything. I'm a princess, you know,
and I'm never allowed to handle money!"
"A princess, indeed . . ." Bagseye's greasy purr grew
even greasier. "In that case, my dear, here's
ANOTHER BAG!"

And with a well-practised swirl, he threw a sack over Camomile, pulled the drawstring, swung her over his shoulder and bundled her upstairs.

Meanwhile, back at the castle, everyone had woken up
to no Princess Camomile and the Queen was screaming,
"WHERE IS SHE?"
"I c..c..can't think," stammered Nanny Nettle.

"She's never allowed . . ."
"Well, it looks like NEVER, HAS!" yelled the King.
"Call the gardener. Call everyone. Search everywhere!
House, grounds and *specially* where she's not allowed!"

And while the royal search party searched, Bagseye rubbed his greasy paws above the sweet shop and untied Camomile's sack.

"Now", he said, "all we have to do is write your father a ransom note demanding a reward for you and I'll be bad *and* rich. Yippee!"

"*We?*" said Camomile. "Can't *you* write?"

"And when would I have learned to write? Or read,

for that matter," snarled Bagseye. "I've been far too
busy studying to be BAD! Now . . . I'll dictate! You write!"
"Hmm," said Camomile thoughtfully. "All right.
On one condition: for every word I write, I get one
of what I'm not allowed."

"Sure," shrugged Bagseye. "Why should I care if all your teeth fall out! Let's get on with it."
So Camomile sat on the floor with paper and pen.
"Off you go!" she said happily.

"Dear King Waldo," dictated Bagseye,
pacing about.

Dear Daddy wrote Camomile cleverly.

"I have your precious daughter,"
dictated Bagseye.

I'm at a place where I'm not allowed called
Bagseye's Sweet Shop wrote Camomile.

"If you want her back leave a huge reward outside
the castle front gates at midnight and I'll leave her
at the back at dawn and no messing about.
Yours, No-One-You-Know"
dictated Bagseye.

But I'm enjoying myself so don't come and get
me for half an hour
Lots of love
C XXXXX

wrote Camomile.

Then she and Bagseye counted up the words as best they could and while Bagseye set off to slip the note under the castle door, Camomile went downstairs to the shop and chose . . .

. . . *three* sugar bears, *four* jelly mice,
two liquorice wheels, *two* sherbet dibdabs,
two sugar plums, *four* marzipan roses,
one chocolate bunny, *one* packet of blueberry
gums, *two* aniseed balls, *four* nougat-nut whirls
and *seven* sugared almonds.

And by the time the King had received the Bagseye note and roared for the Queen who roared for Nanny Nettle . . .

. . . who roared for the gardener who roared for the chauffeur . . .

. . . and they'd all roared down the road,
nearly running over Bagseye . . .

. . . she'd eaten the lot and was feeling very, very SICK!
"Oh dear, oh dear!" said the Queen, scooping her up
gratefully and bundling her home to bed. "But at least
now you know."

"Know what?" said Camomile, weakly.
"That sweets make you sick, Little Madam!" said
Nanny Nettle. "And that's why I never allow them!"

"OH, NO!" said Camomile, throwing back
the covers and jumping out of bed. "It wasn't *sweets*.
It was *too many* sweets — eaten one after the other
because I was so excited about having what I'm not
allowed . . . THAT'S what made me sick!
And that's why I rode my bike where
I wasn't allowed and got bagged by
that bad cat Bagseye!"
"Bagged?" gasped the King
and Queen.
"Yes," said Camomile.
"He was going to send you
a ransom note but he couldn't
write so I did and that's how
I told you where I was."

"Oh, my goodness!" gasped Nanny Nettle.
"What *are* we going to do with her?"
"I know," said the King. "We're going to give her
a little of what she's not allowed!"
"Just a little," said the Queen, "so you don't want
so much you get into trouble."
"Jelly mice, I think," said Camomile.
"And," said the King, "Nanny Nettle is going to
take you for a bike ride every day of the week!"
"But I can't ride a bike!"
gasped Nanny Nettle.
"Then you'll learn,"
said the King.
"We'll all learn,"
said the Queen.

So, true to the King's word, they all learned to ride a bike and, keeping a careful eye out for that bad cat, Bagseye, every day someone took Camomile for a ride on the wild side of the castle walls.

And every week, Nanny Nettle ordered a few sweets
to be delivered from Bullseye the Good Cat's Sweet Shop
in town. And every week Camomile counted them out,

gave Nanny Nettle her share and said,
"Now don't eat them all at once, Nanny Nettle,
whatever you do!"